THE SE~~~~ ~~
LOST KINGDOM

Alistair Nakhai

&

Yasmine Rasti

Printed in the United Kingdom.

For more information, contact:
b2bcontact@gmail.com

Book design by Alistair Nakhai
Cover design by Alistair Nakhai
Content by Yasmine Rasti & Alistair Nakhai

ISBN - Paperback: 9798386508425

First Edition: March 2023

About the Authors

Alistair Nakhai & Yasmine Rasti, the authors of this children's book, have always had a passion for storytelling and a love for nature and animals. Growing up, Alistair & Yasmine spent much of their time exploring the great outdoors, and this experience has shaped their writing.

As an environmentalist and animal lovers, Alistair & Yasmine are committed to creating stories that inspire children to care for the planet and its creatures. They believe that children are the key to building a better future and that by instilling in them a love for nature and wildlife, we can create a more sustainable world.

In addition to their passion for the environment, Alistair & Yasmine are also committed to empowering children with the tools they need to succeed in life. Through their writing, they hope to inspire confidence and self-belief in young readers, encouraging them to follow their dreams and achieve their goals.

Alistair & Yasmine hope that this children's book will not only entertain and delight young readers but also inspire them to care for the environment, respect animals, and believe in themselves.

Acknowledgments

I am deeply thankful to my wife Yasmine Rasti for her unwavering love and support throughout this journey. Her invaluable contributions have not only fueled my inspiration but have also played a pivotal role in transforming the manuscript into the enchanting book it is today. Collaborating with her has been an absolute delight, and I am truly blessed to share this creative adventure with her by my side.

Contents

Chapter 1

A New Life

Amayah was a young girl, living with her cruel stepmother in a small cottage at the edge of the forest. Her life had not been easy, having lost her mother at an early age to illness. Despite her difficult circumstances, Amayah was always able to find a silver lining in every situation. She was kind, optimistic and resilient - a true fighter.

One day, Amayah's stepmother sent her out into the forest to collect some mushrooms for dinner. Amayah had been warned to stay on the path and not to wander, so she reluctantly trudged through the forest, her spirits low.

Suddenly, Amayah heard a noise coming from a clearing. She cautiously approached and was shocked to find a deer fawn caught in a hunter's trap. She quickly freed the fawn, the fawn paused as if it was saying thank you to her and then scampered away into the safety of the trees.

Amayah was about to continue on her way when an owl swooped in from the sky, startling her. It was an enormous bird, its eyes a brilliant shade of golden amber. It alighted on a nearby branch and stared at Amayah intently.

Amayah was mesmerized by the owl, and she felt an instant connection with it. She held out her hand, and the owl flew down to her, landing softly on her arm. Amayah was surprised - she had never seen an owl this close

before.

The owl seemed to sense Amayah's sadness, and it hooted softly at her. Amayah felt a warmth in her heart - she had made a friend. She smiled, and the owl flew away, but she knew it would return.

Amayah finished her task quickly, and made her way home, her spirits lifted. As she walked, she wondered what adventures the owl would lead her on. Little did she know that her life was about to change forever.

The next day, Amayah awoke to find the owl perched on her windowsill. It seemed to be beckoning her to follow, and so Amayah decided to take a chance. She put on her cloak and opened the window, and with a hop, the owl was off into the sky.

Amayah followed the owl's leads, deeper and deeper into the forest. She felt a strange sense of calm as she walked through the trees. She felt a mysterious power within her, like she could do anything.

Suddenly the owl sat on a tree branch and started talking to her. He said to her that he was a guardian spirit and that he saw her saving the deer fawn. He said that she has special powers and that she was the chosen one to save the Lost Kingdom from the hunters and the evil witch who would destroy it and he is here to guide her on her way.

Amayah couldn't believe her ears! She thought she was dreaming, she could actually be speaking to an owl! She felt a warm sensation come over her. So she decided to go with it and follow the owl to see where it was leading her.

Chapter 2

A Night with
the Wolves

Amayah continued her journey deep into the mysterious forest, feeling both nervous and excited. She had heard stories of dangerous animals and other dangers lurking in the shadows, but she was determined to find the Lost Kingdom. Suddenly, she heard a soft whimper, and as she followed the sound, she came across a wolf cub caught in a hunter's trap.

Without hesitation, Amayah sprang into action, using all her strength to free the cub. She had just finished freeing the cub when she heard a loud growl, and as she turned around, she saw a pack of wolves surrounding her. Their red eyes watched her carefully, and Amayah felt fear wash over her. But then, she noticed the mother wolf step forward and nuzzle her cub, expressing gratitude for Amayah's help.

To her surprise, the mother wolf invited her to stay in their den for the night. At first, Amayah was hesitant, but the wolf's kind eyes and gentle demeanour won her over, and she agreed. As she spent the night in the den, Amayah learned all about the wolves and their pack. She discovered that they were a close-knit family, fiercely loyal to one another, and dedicated to their community.

In the morning, as Amayah prepared to continue her journey, the mother wolf presented her with a special necklace, representing the symbol of the

pack. It was the ultimate sign of friendship and loyalty, and Amayah felt deeply touched by the wolves' kindness and generosity. She thanked them and resumed her journey, her heart full of courage and determination, and her spirit strengthened by the lessons she had learned from the wolves.

As she walked through the forest, she felt a new sense of connection with the world around her, and she was filled with a deep appreciation for the wonders of nature. Amayah knew that her journey was far from over, but she was no longer afraid, for she had found friends in the unlikeliest of places, and she had learned the true meaning of trust and loyalty.

Chapter 3

The Trust of the
Majestic Tiger

As Amayah followed the owl deeper into the forest, she couldn't help but feel a sense of wonder and excitement at all the new sights and sounds around her. The leaves rustled in the wind, and the birds sang melodiously in the trees. But her peace was suddenly disturbed by a loud rumble that echoed throughout the forest. The owl flew ahead, and when Amayah turned around, she was face to face with a massive tiger!

The tiger started circling her, and Amayah was about to scream when she noticed that the tiger was limping and had a thorn stuck in its paw. Without hesitation, Amayah jumped forward and removed the thorn from the tiger's paw. The tiger stopped and looked at Amayah with gratitude, then to her surprise, it began licking her face, expressing his thanks.

Amayah was astonished, and the tiger's trust meant the world to her. She thanked the tiger for the immense gift of trust, and the tiger nodded before disappearing back into the forest. With this new-found determination, Amayah continued her journey, eager to explore what lay ahead.

As she walked, she noticed that the animals in the forest were friendlier than before. They would come up to her, nuzzle her hand, or simply watch her with interest. Amayah was starting to realize that the journey was not only about finding the Lost Kingdom but also about discovering herself and the connections she could make with the creatures of the forest.

Amayah was sure the secret Lost Kingdom was close, and her heart raced with excitement at the thought of what lay ahead. With her new friend, the owl, and the memory of the trust she had earned from the majestic tiger, Amayah continued her journey with confidence and determination.

As she walked, she knew that she was not alone on her journey, and she was grateful for the trust and friendship she had found in the forest. Amayah smiled, knowing that she would never forget the lessons she learned from the tiger, and that she would always cherish the trust and friendship she had gained on her journey.

Chapter 4

The Wisdom of
the Merpeople

Amayah was walking through the dense forest when she suddenly heard a distant sound of music and singing. She was curious and decided to follow the sound, leading her to a small lake. She was shocked to see a group of merpeople playing instruments and singing, surrounded by colourful fish and sea creatures. Amayah had heard stories of merpeople, but she never thought she would see them in real life.

She approached the edge of the lake and was about to speak when a mermaid appeared in front of her. The mermaid had long, flowing hair and a shimmering tail. She looked at Amayah with kind eyes and introduced herself as Queen Ariel of the merpeople. Queen Ariel invited Amayah to join the merpeople in their underwater kingdom. Amayah was hesitant at first, but she was fascinated by the merpeople and their culture, so she agreed.

Amayah was amazed at what she saw. The underwater kingdom was breathtaking, with glowing plants and shining stones. The merpeople welcomed Amayah with open arms and showed her their way of life. Amayah learned how they lived in harmony with the sea and all its creatures. She also learned how they used the power of song to communicate with each other and with the sea.

Queen Ariel took Amayah to see the wise old mermaid, who was said to

know the secrets of the sea. The wise old mermaid told Amayah the story of how the merpeople came to be and how they lived in peace with the sea until the hunter and his men came along and camped by the lake and littered the lake. She also told Amayah of the importance of listening to the sea and the creatures that lived in it.

Queen Ariel then gave Amayah a special pearl as a thank you gift. Amayah was so grateful for the gift and the wisdom the merpeople had shared with her and was inspired by their kindness and love for the sea. She realised that she had much to learn from the merpeople and decided to stay with them for a while longer, to learn more about their culture and the sea.

The adventures with the merpeople taught Amayah the importance of living in harmony with the environment and listening to the wisdom of the sea. She left the underwater kingdom with a new appreciation for the ocean and all its creatures and was ready for whatever her next adventure would bring.

Chapter 5

The Lost Kingdom

Amayah's journey took her deeper into the heart of the forest, her heart pounding with excitement and anticipation. She followed the owl as it led her towards a massive waterfall, the sound of the cascading water growing louder with each step. As she approached, she noticed a small cave hidden behind the waterfall and her heart skipped a beat. Could this be the entrance to the Lost Kingdom?

Determined to find out, Amayah made her way into the cave, drenched from the spray of the waterfall but filled with excitement. As she explored the dark and damp cave, she felt a sense of wonder and magic surrounding her. Suddenly, she heard the sound of music and laughter, coming from deeper in the cave.

Amayah followed the sounds and found herself in a beautiful and lush world filled with enchanted creatures, colourful flowers and sparkling rivers. She was in awe as she took in the sights and sounds of the Lost Kingdom. Suddenly, she was greeted by a friendly unicorn who offered to give her a tour.

As she explored the kingdom with the unicorn, Amayah met magical creatures of all shapes and sizes, and learned about the rich history and culture of the kingdom. She was amazed by the beauty of the place, and touched by the kindness of the creatures that lived there.

Eventually, Amayah made her way to the heart of the kingdom where she met the Queen, who welcomed her warmly. The Queen told Amayah that the Lost Kingdom was in danger, as an evil witch had cast a spell on the Kingdom, causing black cloud gradually covering the land and the magical creatures to fall into a deep sleep forever. The only way to break the spell was to find the missing three magical Crystals that had been stolen by the witch.

Amayah knew she had to help, and with the support of the Queen and the creatures of the Kingdom, she set out on a quest to find the missing Crystals and save the Lost Kingdom. The journey was filled with adventure and danger, but Amayah's determination and courage never wavered.

Chapter 6

The Crystal Quest

Amayah was determined to find the Crystals and bring it back to the Lost Kingdom, but she didn't know where to start. The owl had flown ahead of her and she was walking through the dense forest when she suddenly heard a loud growl. She stopped and looked around, only to see a massive and angry Minotaur blocking her path.

The Minotaur was roaring and snarling, and Amayah realized that it was guarding the entrance to a cave. She knew that the Crystal must be inside the cave, but she was hesitant to face the Minotaur alone.

Just when she was about to turn around and look for another way, she heard a familiar growl. It was the majestic tiger from the forest of trust, and it was coming to her aid. Amayah felt a wave of relief wash over her, and she ran to the tiger, hugging its neck in gratitude.

Together, Amayah and the tiger approached the Minotaur, who was still growling and snarling. But the tiger didn't back down. It stood its ground, roaring back at the Minotaur and jumped on it and pushed him on to the ground, and the Minotaur eventually stepped aside, allowing Amayah and the tiger to enter the cave.

The inside of the cave was dark and damp, but Amayah could see a glimmer of light in the distance. She followed the light, with the tiger leading

the way, and she soon found herself in a large room filled with glittering jewels and precious stones. And in the centre of the room was a Crystal of immense beauty, glowing with a warm light.

Amayah approached the Crystal mesmerized as she got closer, but she was stopped by a powerful and mysterious being. The being told Amayah that she couldn't take the Crystal, for it was protected and guarded by a powerful spell.

But the tiger didn't give up. It stepped forward, roaring at the mysterious being, and the being finally relented. It told Amayah that she could only take the Crystal if she could replace it with a special pearl that could only be found in the lake guarded by the merpeople. Amayah suddenly remembered the pearl that she was gifted by the merpeople queen so she replaced it with the Crystal and emerged victorious.

As she was holding the Crystal in her hand, the Crystal spoke to her in a soft voice, telling her that it was the key to save the Lost Kingdom. It said that she was the chosen one, and that she had to find the other two Crystals in order to unlock the secrets of the Lost Kingdom and destroy the evil witch.

Amayah was stunned. She had never heard of anything like this before. But she was determined to find the other Crystals and unlock the secrets of the Lost Kingdom.

She took the Crystal and put it in her pocket, and then she set off on a new adventure. She was on a quest to find the other Crystals and unlock the secrets of the Lost Kingdom. She felt brave and strong, and she was sure that she could do it.

As she walked out of the cave, she thanked the tiger for its unwavering support and friendship. She hugged the tiger, and the two of them parted from each other with a deeper bond of friendship and trust.

Few more steps and she saw the owl flying above her. She smiled, knowing that the owl was leading her to the other Crystals. She followed it, and the journey continued.

Chapter 7

The Friendship of
the Centaurs

Amayah continued her journey through the mysterious forest, following the owl and her instincts. Suddenly, she heard the sounds of hooves pounding against the ground, and she froze in fear. She thought it might be the hunters who had been chasing her, but to her surprise, she saw a group of magnificent creatures galloping towards her. They were centaurs, half-human and half-horse, and they were like nothing she had ever seen before.

Amayah felt intimidated by their size and strength, but she didn't let her fear show. She stepped forward and introduced herself, hoping they would be friendly. To her relief, the centaurs smiled and welcomed her into their group. They told her they had been waiting for her, as they had heard of the brave young girl who had saved the wolf cub from the hunter's trap. They admired her courage and wanted to reward her for her kindness.

The centaurs invited Amayah to join them on a journey to the top of a nearby mountain, where they kept their most precious treasure. They said that only the bravest and most deserving individuals were allowed to see it. Amayah was thrilled to be given this opportunity, and she eagerly accepted their invitation.

As they began their climb up the mountain, the centaurs warned Amayah of the dangers that lay ahead. The path was treacherous, and there were

many obstacles along the way. But Amayah didn't back down, and she showed her bravery as she navigated the steep cliffs and dangerous ledges.

Finally, they reached the top of the mountain, and the centaurs revealed their treasure to Amayah. It was a Golden Key that shone like a star, and it was said to have immense power. The centaurs told Amayah that the Golden Key would only reveal its power to someone who was pure of heart and deserving of its gift. They said that she was that person, and they presented the Golden Key to her as a symbol of their friendship and gratitude.

Amayah was overwhelmed by the centaurs' kindness and generosity, and she thanked them from the bottom of her heart. She put the Golden Key in her bag, feeling its weight and its warmth. She knew that this was a treasure unlike any other, and that it would be with her on her journey to the Lost Kingdom.

As she turned to leave, the centaurs wished her luck on her quest and told her that they would always be there for her if she needed their help. Amayah felt the warmth of their friendship and knew that she had made some truly incredible friends on her journey. With her heart full of gratitude, she set off to continue her adventure, determined to reach the Lost Kingdom and find the answers she was seeking.

Chapter 8

The Adventures
with the Unicorns

Amayah continued her journey through the magical forest with the owl leading the way. She was filled with wonder and excitement as she encountered creatures she had never seen before. Suddenly, she heard the soft sounds of a musical instrument, and she realized she was near a clearing.

As she stepped into the clearing, she saw a herd of unicorns playing a melody on their horns. The unicorns were playing a beautiful tune that filled Amayah's heart with joy. She approached the unicorns cautiously, not wanting to startle them. But as she drew near, the unicorns welcomed her with open arms.

One of the unicorns, a beautiful white stallion with a silver horn, stepped forward and introduced himself as the leader of the herd. He told Amayah that he had been waiting for her, and that she had a special mission to complete. The leader explained that the unicorns were in need of help, as a dark force had taken hold of the forest, and they needed Amayah to help defeat it.

Amayah was shocked but also excited. She had never felt more alive and ready for adventure. The leader of the unicorns told her that she would need to find the "Crystal of the Forest," a powerful artefact that would give her the strength to defeat the dark force. The Crystal was located deep in

the River of Treasures and only Amayah could find it.

With the help of the unicorns, Amayah set out on a new adventure to find the Crystal. The journey was full of obstacles and challenges, but Amayah was determined to succeed. She encountered fierce beasts, treacherous terrain, and dark magic, but with her courage and determination, she set out in search of the Crystal.

Chapter 9

The River of Treasures

Amayah continued her journey through the enchanted forest, guided by the wise old owl. She soon came upon a river and was amazed at the sparkling diamonds and gold that lay at the bottom. She couldn't believe her eyes and felt like she had struck a treasure trove. She was eager to explore the river and collect some of the sparkling riches.

As she waded into the water, she suddenly felt herself being pulled under by a strong current. She struggled to keep her head above water, but the current was too strong. Just as she was about to lose consciousness, a friendly otter appeared and offered to help her. The otter told her that the river was known as the River of Treasures and that it was protected by a powerful underwater creature known as the Sea Serpent.

Amayah was sceptical but decided to trust the otter and followed her down into the depths of the river. There she encountered the Sea Serpent, a massive creature with glittering scales and piercing eyes. The Sea Serpent asked her why she was there, and Amayah told the truth, that she was there to collect the riches of the river.

The Sea Serpent laughed and told her that the river's riches were not for the taking. They were to be protected and only given to those who were worthy and pure of heart. Amayah was determined to prove herself worthy and so she set out on a series of challenging tasks, determined to earn

the right to the treasures of the River of Treasures.

With the help of her new friend the otter, Amayah navigated her way through the tasks and soon proved herself to be brave, kind, and wise. The Sea Serpent was impressed and offered her the Crystal of the river as a reward for her bravery and determination. Amayah was overjoyed and thanked the Sea Serpent for the gift.

With second Crystal in hand, Amayah continued her journey, eager to discover the secrets of the Lost Kingdom and eager to find her place in this magical world. She was filled with a sense of adventure and a desire to continue exploring the unknown, always guided by the wisdom of her friend the owl and her new-found friends from the enchanted forest in search of the third and the final Crystal.

Chapter 10

The Courage of the Dragons

Amayah had finally arrived at the entrance to the Crystal Palace, the place where the fabled Crystal of the Lost Kingdom was said to reside. The journey had been long and treacherous, but she was finally here. She had come so far and she was determined to find the Crystal.

As she approached the entrance, she was greeted by two massive dragon guardians. The dragons were breathing fire and their eyes were fierce. Amayah knew she had to be brave if she wanted to enter the palace.

"Who are you and what is your purpose?" the dragons boomed in unison.

Amayah took a deep breath and replied, "I am Amayah, and I am here to find the Crystal of the Lost Kingdom. It is said that it has the power to save the kingdom and bring peace to the land."

The dragons looked at each other and then back at Amayah. "The Crystal of the Lost Kingdom is protected by powerful magic and only the bravest and most worthy can enter the palace."

Amayah didn't falter. She knew she was brave and she knew she was worthy. She stood tall and looked the dragons in the eyes. "I am brave and I am worthy. I have come this far and I will not turn back now."

The dragons were impressed by Amayah's bravery and determination but said that you can only enter if you have a Golden Key. Amayah suddenly remembered the Golden Key that was given to her by the centaurs and pulled it out from around her neck and shouted "here you are, is this what you are looking for?". To their surprise the dragons nodded their heads and stepped aside, allowing her to enter the palace. "You may pass," they said, "but be warned, the journey ahead is filled with dangers and obstacles. Only the bravest will make it to the Crystal."

Amayah entered the palace and the doors closed behind her. She was surrounded by darkness, but she could sense that the Crystal was close. She took a step forward and the ground beneath her feet lit up, illuminating the path ahead.

Amayah's heart was racing as she continued down the path. She encountered countless obstacles and challenges, but she never lost hope. She was determined to find the Crystal and save the kingdom.

Finally, after what felt like an eternity, Amayah saw a glimmer of light in the distance. She quickened her pace and soon she was standing in front of a massive Crystal. It was beautiful, and it was shining with a brilliant light.

Amayah reached out and touched the Crystal. As soon as her fingers made contact, she was filled with a sense of power and peace. She knew she had found what she was looking for. She had found the final Crystal of the Lost Kingdom.

With the Crystal in her hand, Amayah made her way back through the palace and out into the bright sunshine. She knew her journey was far from over, but she was filled with a new sense of courage and determination. She would face any challenge that lay ahead and she would save the kingdom. The courage of the dragons was now within her, and nothing would stop her.

With all three Crystals finally recovered, Amayah returned to the kingdom and placed it back in its rightful place. The spell was broken, and the kingdom was awakened from its slumber. The creatures cheered and celebrated, grateful for Amayah's bravery and selflessness.

Amayah was hailed as a hero, and the Queen honoured her with the title of "Protector of the Lost Kingdom" and gifted her with a very special

gem. Amayah was overjoyed, but she knew that her journey was far from over. With the new friends and skills she had gained, she was ready to face any challenge that lay ahead.

Chapter 11

Returning Home
with a Purpose

As Amayah begins her journey back home, she feels a sense of accomplishment and joy for all the friendships she has made and the knowledge she has gained from the various creatures of the forest. However, her peaceful journey is abruptly interrupted as she suddenly comes face to face with the hunter and his men.

Amayah quickly tries to run, but she soon realizes that there is no escape as the hunter and his men catch up to her. They capture her and tie her up, planning to take her to their village to sell her to the highest bidder. Amayah feels helpless and alone, wondering if she will ever see her family and friends again.

Just when all seems lost, Amayah hears a familiar howl in the distance. It is the wolves who she had helped before. They come to her rescue, howling fiercely and scaring the hunter and his men for good. The wolves surround Amayah, protecting her from any harm.

As Amayah watches the hunter and his men retreat, she realizes that she has a new-found purpose - to protect the creatures of the forest from harm and make it a safer place for all. With the help of her new friends, she knows that she can accomplish anything she sets her mind to.

Amayah had finally reached the end of her journey. The magical world was full of wonders and lessons that she would never forget. She had formed unbreakable bonds with creatures of all shapes and sizes, each of them having taught her something valuable about herself and the world around her. She had discovered a purpose and a direction, and she was eager to return home to share what she had learned with others.

As she walked back through the forest, the owl flew down from a branch and landed on her shoulder, and the mother wolf appeared from the shadows, the wolf cub at her feet.

Amayah thanked them for their help and friendship, and she promised to return one day to visit. She then turned and began to walk down the path that would take her back to her home.

As she walked, she felt a weight lifting from her chest. She had been carrying the burden of her own doubts and fears, but the creatures of the Lost Kingdom had shown her that she was capable of more than she ever imagined. She had discovered her own courage and the strength of her own heart.

When Amayah finally emerged from the forest, she found her stepmother waiting for her. At first she was upset with her going without her permission, but when she listened intently as she shared her stories of adventure and self-discovery, her stepmother was amazed by the lessons she had learned and the friends she had made. She saw the confidence and determination in her eyes, and she was proud of the young woman she had become.

Amayah returned home with a purpose, determined to use the wisdom she had gained to help others. She knew that she had the courage to face any challenge that came her way and that she had the strength to overcome it. With a smile on her face and a light in her heart, Amayah knew that she was ready for whatever adventures lay ahead.

Printed in Great Britain
by Amazon

20441603R00031